AN ORIGIN STORY

by Scott Peterson

based on the story by Stan Lee and Steve Ditko

www.marvel.com

TM & © 2011 Marvel & Subs.

Published by Scholastic Australia in 2012.
Scholastic Australia Pty Limited PO Box 579 Gosford NSW 2250 ABN 11 000 614 577 www.scholastic.com.au

Part of the Scholastic Group
Sydney • Auckland • New York • Toronto • London • Mexico City • New Delhi • Hong Kong • Buenos Aires • Puerto Rico

All rights reserved. No part of this publication may be reproduced or transmitted in any form or by any means, electronic or mechanical, including photocopying, recording, storage in an information retrieval system, or otherwise, without the prior written permission of the publisher, unless specifically permitted under the Australian Copyright Act 1968 as amended.

ISBN 978-1-74283-234-0

Printed in China by RR Donnelley

10 9 8 7 6 5 4 3 2 1   12 13 14 15 16 / 2

CHAPTER 1

It's no fun having no friends.

Peter Parker knew all about that.

He hadn't had a real friend since he'd started school.

Maybe it was because he always got the best grades in the class. Maybe it was because he wasn't very big or strong or handsome.

It made him sad sometimes. But his life wasn't all bad.

For one thing, he really did love school—especially

science.

And Peter loved cameras. He loved taking photographs. And, as with science, he was good at it.

Most of all, he had his Uncle Ben and Aunt May.

Peter lived with his aunt and uncle; they had raised him since he was a baby. They gave him all the love any child could ever want or need. They were his favourite people in the world, and he thought they were just perfect.

His home in Queens, New York was small, but it was clean and neat and comfortable. Peter loved everything about it.

Which was good, since school was so hard. No one wanted to talk to him in class and he  had no one to sit with at lunch. Most of the day he was ignored. But it was even worse when he wasn't.

Some of the boys who played on the football team liked to push him around, and they were all so much bigger and stronger than Peter that there was nothing he could do about it.

It was hard. But Peter had science and photography. And most of all he had his family.

And he had a trip to the Science Hall to look forward to. He couldn't wait.

CHAPTER 2

The Science Hall was one of Peter's favourite places in the world—an entire building full of people just like him: people who loved science. Everywhere he looked, there were exciting lab tests and experiments going on. He couldn't get enough of the place.

No one else in his class felt the same way. Peter had been so happy to learn about the new exhibit at the hall. It was about radioactivity, and Peter was so excited, he did something he didn't do very often: he went out of his way to talk to his classmates.

Peter was sure that even people not interested in science would want to go if they heard.

'Are you kidding?'

'I don't *think* so.'

'Radio-what?'

No one wanted to go. So, as usual, Peter went by himself.

'And now,' Peter heard one of the scientists saying, 'for a demonstration of how we can control radioactive rays in the laboratory.'

Peter jostled for position. He *had* to see this! He knew if something was radio-active, it meant its atoms were unstable. Atoms were much, much too small to see, and everything in the entire universe was made up of them. The idea of something that important being both that small and dangerously unstable? Peter was all over that.

As Peter tried to push closer to get a better view, he felt something on his hand. Without thinking, he tried to shake it off.

'Ow!'

Peter didn't notice the people turning to look at

him, annoyed at his interrupting the speaker. He was too busy looking at his own hand.

It hurt. It hurt a lot. In fact, it felt like it was burning. But that wasn't the weirdest thing.

There was a spider on his hand. A *glowing* spider. Peter gave a cry and shook the spider off. The spider had bitten him. He could see the puncture marks, and his hand was starting to swell.

Peter swayed. He felt strange—he was

dizzy and his vision was blurry. Every- thing sounded strange too— much too loud one moment and then almost silent the next. And he had a nasty taste in his mouth.

'Peter? Are you all right?'

Peter looked around. Some of the scientists were looking at him. They seemed worried.

'I...I need some air,' he mumbled.

Peter stumbled outside. He hadn't realized how hot he was until he felt the crisp, refreshing air on his face.

Suddenly, Peter started shaking. His legs felt like they wouldn't hold up much longer, but there was nowhere to sit. He stumbled forward, fighting for balance.

Between his worries and how sick he felt, Peter didn't pay attention to where he was going.

Which is why he walked right into the street without looking.

CHAPTER 3

Peter didn't see the car zooming towards him.
He didn't even hear the car honking.

But just before the car would have hit him, Peter suddenly got the urge to *jump*.

It was a strange thing to suddenly want to do. But the feeling was so powerful, that Peter had no choice.

Peter jumped.

He jumped higher than he had ever jumped before—higher than he had ever seen *anyone* jump in his whole life. He bounded into the air above the rushing car. It passed under him, whooshing beneath his feet.

The whole thing happened so fast he hardly even had time to draw a breath. *How did I do that?* he thought. *I didn't even know that car was coming.*

That was when he looked down.

Peter was clinging to the side of a building.

This was impossible!

He shook his head, wondering if he were dreaming. He looked down again.

He was still three metres off the ground. Stuck to the side of the building. Without even trying.

Still feeling like he was in a dream, Peter began to climb.

He went up the side of the building as easily as he'd walked to the kitchen that morning, it seemed as though his hands just stuck to the bricks of the building. But they *weren't* sticky—they came right off, without feeling like there was any glue on them.

In seconds, Peter was at the top of the building. He grabbed a steel drainpipe and without even meaning to, crushed it as though it were a paper cup.

How is this happening, Peter wondered.

Peter looked out over the city. 'Well,' he said, 'At least I'm feeling better now. I guess that spider bite...'

And that's when he knew.

The spider. The *glowing* spider.

It has to be the spider bite, Peter thought.

Somehow…when it bit me, it…it transferred its powers to me.

Peter laughed. That wasn't really possible. Was it?

He couldn't deny that he'd climbed the wall like…well, like a spider. He'd jumped like a spider. And there was no way he'd have been able to even dent steel yesterday, much less crush it.

Spiders were known to be remarkably strong for their size, he thought.

You're a scientist. Run an experiment.

Peter made sure no one was watching, then went over to a car parked nearby. He tried lifting it. He didn't think he'd be able to push an entire car over…but he didn't want to hurt someone's car, either, just in case he was that strong.

He was that strong.

Peter stood the car on its rear wheels as easily as he carried laundry upstairs for Aunt May.

Excited, he rushed over to a truck. He slid underneath.

'Ugh,' he said, thinking of how dirty his clothes were probably getting. Well, it was all in the name of science.

Lying flat on the alley floor, Peter put his hands on the underside of the truck and pushed up.

It was like lifting a pillow.

I have the powers of a spider, he thought. *It's impossible. And yet it's true. I'm a scientist, and I have to face the facts, no matter how amazing they seem.*

And, he thought, *that's just the word for it: amazing.*

I have the powers of a spider.

CHAPTER 4

Peter walked down the street in a daze.

He was so confused by everything that had happened, he didn't notice where he was walking.

'Hey!' someone yelled. 'Watch it, pal!'

Peter looked up. He was surprised to find himself in a crowd of people.

He glanced around, and saw he was in front of a theatre.

There was a sign on the window. *Today! The best wrestling in town!*

He started to walk away, then stopped.

There was another sign he hadn't noticed. And this one said, *$1,000 to the man who can stay in the ring three minutes with Crusher Hogan.*

A thousand dollars.

Peter had never had even half that much money in his life! With his new powers, maybe he could...could he?

There was one way to find out.

He rushed home. He didn't think anyone there would be likely to recognize Peter Parker the bookworm in such an unlikely place. But it was better not to take chances. 'I'll put on some old clothes,' he said. 'And—'

He looked around the room. He could see. He had taken his glasses off to change his shirt and yet...he could still see. Even without his glasses. He hadn't been able to see without his glasses since he was a little kid.

'—and leave my glasses here,' he said. He smiled.

He scratched his head. 'I'll find some way to disguise myself...'

Peter grabbed an old bandana. He held it up to the light. It was so thin he could see through it—at least, he could now that he had perfect vision. But with it tied around his face,

there was no way anyone there would ever be able to tell who he really was.

A few minutes later, Peter was standing near the wrestling ring. An enormous bald man was holding another man over his head... using just one arm. The crowd began to chant.

'Crusher! Crusher! Crusher!'

The bald man grinned. Then he slammed the other man down to the mat. The man was still, and clearly unconscious.

The crowd went crazy. 'Crusher! Crusher! Crusher!' they screamed.

Well, I guess that's Crusher, Peter thought. *I guess that's my...opponent.*

'Who's next?' Crusher yelled. 'Where's my next victim?'

As the crowd continued to chant, Peter looked around.

This is crazy, he thought. But he stepped

forward anyway.

His voice shook as he said, 'I'll try for that thousand dollars.'

The crowd grew quiet. Crusher stared at Peter. Then he began to laugh. Soon the whole crowd was laughing.

'Well, well,' he said. 'If it ain't a little masked marvel.'

As Peter climbed into the wrestling ring, Crusher said, 'Now just relax, Shorty.' He cracked his knuckles. 'I'll try to make this as painless as possible.'

Crusher suddenly ran forward. Peter barely had time to think *and fast!* before the big man was on him.

Without even thinking, Peter leapt up in the air. Putting his hands on the top of Crusher's head, he leapfrogged over the wrestler.

Peter landed and turned around. The move had surprised Crusher so much, the man had tripped and fallen on his face. He got up slowly. And he wasn't laughing any more.

Now he looked *mad.*

Uh-oh, Peter thought.

Crusher rushed towards Peter again. This time, Peter slid *underneath* Crusher, between his feet. By the time Peter turned around to face the big man, the wrestler had already turned around himself.

This time, Crusher didn't run—he walked towards Peter. His arms were spread wide, cutting off Peter's escape.

His eyes still on Crusher, Peter climbed up onto the top the rope. 'What are you going to do now?' Crusher asked. 'If you leave the ring, you lose. No money for you.'

Crusher ran at Peter, his hands in front of him. *He wants to push me off the rope and into the crowd,* Peter thought. *Huh. He's not trying to hurt me anymore. Now he just wants this to be over.*

Something occurred to Peter. *He...he's afraid he can't win.*

That huge guy is afraid of me.

As the wrestler grabbed for him, Peter darted to the side, then kept going. He ran around the ring on the rope as if it were nothing. Crusher tried and tried to grab him, but Peter was too fast.

The crowd had been cheering for Crusher, but many were now starting to root for Peter.

'Who *is* that kid?' Peter heard someone say. 'He's amazing!'

Crusher was getting angrier by the second, but he didn't know what to do.

'Hey!' he shouted to Peter. 'Stop running! Or are you too afraid to face me?'

'Not too afraid,' Peter called back. 'Too smart!'

Peter stopped. 'But...okay,' he said. 'If you

insist. We can do it your way.'

He jumped down to the middle of the ring. Crusher didn't move—he couldn't figure out what to do next. With this kid, it seemed like anything was possible.

So Peter moved. He circled Crusher again and again, the big man turning and turning to keep Peter in sight. Soon the wrestler was dizzy.

Peter darted in and lifted Crusher onto his shoulder. The crowd gasped.

'Is he really doing that?'

'I can't believe it!'

'You ever seen anything like this?'

With Crusher on his shoulder, Peter climbed the pole in one of the ring's four corners. *I'm stronger,* Peter thought. *Let's see just how* much *stronger.*

Peter climbed to the top of the pole and

stood with Crusher balanced over his head. The wrestler started yelling, 'Put me *down!* You win! *You win!'*

The grew silent. Then cheers burst forth.

He held Crusher above his head. With one hand under the wrestler's chest, Peter grabbed one of Crusher's feet with his other hand... then spun the man around like a top.

The crowd screamed with delight. Peter stopped when Crusher began to sound like he might throw up. *That* was something spider powers wouldn't be able to help with.

As Peter sat Crusher back down in the ring, the referee called, 'And we have a winner! The masked marvel defeats Crusher Hogan!'

'You—you're not *human*,' Crusher said to Peter. Peter was the only one who heard, but everyone could see the fear on Crusher's face. '*Nobody* can do that.'

Peter laughed. 'Wanna bet?'

CHAPTER 5

'Eight hundred...nine hundred...and one thousand,' the promoter said. He didn't smile as he handed Peter a stack of bills. 'There you go, pal. That's the first time I've ever had to pay anyone for fighting Crusher—most people get taken away by an ambulance.'

As Peter moved left the theatre, he could hear people still talking about him.

'Greatest act I've ever seen!'

'Sensational!'

'Fantastic!'

'He was terrific!'

'Friend!' a voice called out. 'Hey, friend!'

Peter turned around. A man in a tie waved to him. 'Listen, friend,' the man said. 'I'm a television producer, and with that act of yours, I can make you a fortune. You hear me?'

Peter opened his mouth to reply, but the man kept speaking quickly.

'And keep the mask angle—it's great showmanship!' He put something in Peter's hand. 'Here's my business card—call me. I can get you on all the most popular shows. You'd be a smash!'

'Thanks…' Peter said, his head spinning. A television star? Him? Plain ol' Peter Parker?

He looked at the money he'd made wrestling. It was more than he'd ever had, but that man had said he could get Peter even more.

And maybe if he were on television…maybe people would finally like him.

Peter made his way home. His aunt and uncle were in the kitchen.

'Hello, dear,' Aunt May said.

'What's doin', Pete?' Uncle Ben asked.

'Um…' Peter said. How could he possibly explain all that had happened that day? Peter wasn't sure himself. 'I…I think I'm going to go up to my room for a bit,' he mumbled.

Peter sat on his bed, then stood back up; he was too excited and confused to be still—too much had happened to him.

He looked at himself in the mirror. He didn't look different. He still looked like Peter Parker.

Peter Parker. The man had said he couldn't just be himself—he'd said Peter should stick with a mask. But surely he could do better than that old bandana.

He needed a costume.

But what kind of costume? *Well,* Peter thought. *You got bit by a spider, and you've got the powers of a spider. Why not a costume to match?*

Peter grabbed a piece of paper and a pencil and drew a quick sketch. 'That'll work,' he said.

He found some old material and got to work, cutting and sewing.

Then something occurred to him. 'I've got the speed of a spider, and the strength of a spider. And I can climb walls like a spider. But

I don't have a spider's web.'

He pulled out his chemistry set. After some tricky work, he

had a liquid that was as sticky and strong as a spider's web. *And I can wear these web-shooters around my wrist,* he thought. *They'll hold the webbing as a liquid, until I move my finger like this and...*

Zip. A web shot out. It stuck to the ceiling. Peter swung himself around on it. 'Perfect!' he said.

After his aunt and uncle had gone to bed, Peter finished up his costume. He tried it on.

'Yup,' he said, looking at it. 'That'll do. It's thin enough that I can wear it underneath my clothes...well, without the mask, at least. I—'

He stopped. He had a costume to go with his new powers. But he needed a name to go with his new costume.

'Okay, world,' he said. 'Here comes... SPIDER-MAN!'

CHAPTER 6

'You've heard about him. And now, ladies and gentlemen, here he is: the amazing Spider-Man!'

Peter walked out on stage. Television cameras moved all around, trying to get the perfect shot of this new character everyone was talking about.

'So, Spidey,' the television host said. 'Can I, can I call you "Spidey"?'

Peter—Spider-Man—laughed. 'I've been called worse.'

The audience laughed along. Peter was

startled. He'd never had anyone but his aunt and uncle laugh at his jokes before.

It felt good.

'Well, all right,' the host said. 'What are you going to show us?'

'How about this?' Peter asked. He walked over to the wall and put one foot on it. Then he walked straight up the wall as though it were just a little hill.

He shot a web to the ceiling over the audience's head, then swung right over them. Some screamed, some tried to touch him and many clapped.

Peter hung upside down. He shot a web towards the stage. It hit the water bottle next to the host. Peter

gave it a hard pull and the water bottle zipped towards him. He caught it easily and started to take a drink, then stopped.

'Have to remember to add a mouth to this mask,' he said, and the audience laughed again.

Peter walked across the ceiling, upside down, until he was over the host's desk. 'Okay, Spider-Man,' he heard the producer say. 'That's enough! Don't show 'em too much!'

Peter dropped to the stage, gave a short bow and a quick wave, and ran off stage.

The producer came over. As the audience called for more, the producer said, 'First rule of show business: always leave 'em beggin' for more.'

They walked out of the studio and headed for the building's elevator. 'There he is!' someone called. People rushed over.

'I'm from Newstime magazine! We'll pay you anything you want for an interview!'

'No! Sign with me—I can get you a movie deal!'

'Wait! Please! Just a quick photograph!'

Peter didn't even slow down. 'See my agent, folks. I'm busy.'

So this is fame, Peter thought. *This part isn't as great as I'd thought it would be.*

'Stop! Stop him!'

Oh, what now? Peter thought, as he pushed the button for the lift. He didn't even look up— he was already getting tired of people asking him for things.

'If he makes it to the lift,' the voice yelled. 'He'll get away!'

Peter rolled his eyes. The lift doors opened.

A heavy blond man raced by. Peter watched as he jumped into the lift. 'Made it!' the man yelled.

Peter turned to see a police officer running towards them. The cop reached out…but the doors closed too soon.

Just before the lift closed all the way, the blond man looked right at Peter. He nodded gratefully.

The policeman punched the closed lift door in frustration. Then he turned on Peter.

'What's *with* you, mister?' he shouted. 'All you had to do was trip him! Or even just hold him for a second!'

'Sorry,' Peter shrugged. 'That's *your* job.'

The cop's face turned red with anger. 'I ought to arrest you.'

CHAPTER 7

When Peter got home that night, his aunt and uncle were waiting for him.

'Peter,' Aunt May said. Peter's heart sank. She looked so *serious,* standing there with her hands behind her back. So formal. They both did.

Did they know about Spider-Man? Could they possibly have found out? Had they seen him on television and recognized his voice?

'You know that microscope

you've always wanted?' she asked. Peter blinked. 'Your uncle and I bought it for you this afternoon!'

Aunt May brought her hands out from behind her back and handed the microscope to him.

He looked at the microscope. They must have saved for so long. And this gift, for no reason—they just bought it for him because they loved him.

That night, lying in bed, Peter thought over the day's events. *Aunt May and Uncle Ben are the only ones who've ever been kind to me.*

His manager had gotten him a spot on one of the most popular television shows. Its host was Alan Stephens. Peter was very excited—but things started to go wrong almost right away. When Spider-Man was introduced, Peter walked out on stage. Also on stage were dozens of big spider dolls.

'Well, well, well,' Alan said. 'So you're really real—the human spider.'

Peter nodded.

'Tell me,' Alan said. 'Spiders—they're bugs, right?'

'Uh...' Peter said. He hadn't been expecting this—he'd thought he would just do some more tricks. 'Technically spiders are arthropods. They—'

'Hey!' Alan said, turning to his guests. 'It not only speaks, it's an educated insect. If that doesn't beat all.'

The guests laughed. So did the audience.

Peter chuckled too, but he felt uneasy. When were they going to get to the tricks?

It's...it's not supposed to be like this, he thought. *This isn't supposed to be happening. I have these amazing powers.*

People aren't supposed to make fun of me anymore.

'So now it's time for a little song and dance,' the host said. 'I think a duet would be great, don't you?'

The crowd cheered as the singer stood up. Someone handed Peter a microphone.

'Wait,' he said. 'You want *me* to sing? But… but I don't…'

The band started playing 'The Itsy-Bitsy Spider.' *Right,* Peter thought to himself. *Even I can sing this song.*

But suddenly the band started playing faster, and the beat was different. The singer smiled sadly at Peter, then started singing a jazzy version of the song.

It was the longest two minutes of Peter's life.

Later, when the show was finally over, Peter

tried to slink away.

'Have a good time?'

Peter turned around. Alan Stephens was walking towards him. 'Not quite what you'd expected?'

'Why?' Peter asked. 'Why did you do that? What'd I do to you?'

The host shrugged. 'Nothing. You didn't do anything to me. Or *for* me. But your agent, now...he charged us a fortune to get you on here.' He pointed at Peter. 'You like that part, right? You like the money? Well, bug-man, everything comes with a price. If you want to play with the big boys, you better get tough. That's how it is in this game.'

As Peter watched him walk away, he thought to himself. *Everything has a price. Well, I'm not sure I like this game enough to pay that price.*

CHAPTER 8

Peter's agent had booked him on more shows. But after that, Peter made sure they were all recorded—no more live shows for him.

But Peter found himself having less and less fun and he didn't like the way people were looking to use him, either.

Peter had just finished another show and was leaving when someone called after him.

He almost didn't stop, or even turn around. But he hesitated. Something about the voice sounded different from most of the people he met.

Peter looked behind him and saw a man waving at him. He was standing next to a little girl in a wheelchair.

'Please,' the man said. 'One minute of your time? My girl just wants to meet you. This is my daughter, Tanisha,' the man said.

Peter squatted down next to her wheelchair. 'Hi,' he said.

She looked up at him with big eyes. 'It's you,' she whispered. 'It's really you.'

'Thank you,' the man said. 'You're all she talks about these days. You're her hero.'

Peter's throat closed up. No one had ever looked up to him before. His aunt and uncle loved him. Some of the crowds clapped for him. But he had never been anyone's hero before.

He smiled underneath his mask. *Hero.* Wow. He liked that. That felt good.

'Well,' he said. 'I don't know that I deserve

that. But…'

Peter grabbed her hand. 'I'm very glad to meet you.'

Tanisha looked up at him with tears in her eyes. Peter didn't think he'd ever seen anything more beautiful than the smile that broke out on her face.

'Hey,' he said. 'Would you like to go for a ride?'

He stopped and turned to her father. 'I mean…is that okay? Can she—'

Her father grinned. 'That would be wonderful? But are you sure? I mean, I'm sure you're very busy and all.'

Peter laughed. 'I'm never too busy for my fans. Well…for my *fan*.'

He picked the little girl up. He carried her back into the studio, her father following right behind. Everyone else was gone.

'Perfect,' he said. 'Tell me when you want me to put you back down.'

He climbed up walls with her, hung from the ceiling, and swung from one end of the studio to the other. 'Sure you want me to keep going?' he kept asking. And every time she would just laugh, 'Yes! More! More!'

Finally, he brought her back down to her father.

Her father shook Spider-Man's hand, then suddenly grabbed him and gave him a bear hug. 'Thank you,' he said again. 'I can't tell you how much this means.'

Peter looked down at Tanisha sitting in her wheelchair. Her face was glowing with joy. Peter smiled.

'You know, I think I have an idea.'

CHAPTER 9

There was a police car outside his house.

Peter froze. Why were the police at his house?

Was it about Spider-Man?

No, he decided. It couldn't be about Spider-Man—he'd only been concerned about himself: he couldn't have done anything wrong.

Peter made sure his costume wasn't visible under his clothes. The he opened the front door.

He heard something—but, no, that was coming from next door. Was it…was someone crying? Peter thought for a moment it might have sounded a little like Aunt May. But it couldn't be. He'd never heard Aunt May cry before.

'Oh, hey,' a voice said.

A police officer come out of the kitchen. He walked over and put a hand on Peter's shoulder. The man took a deep breath.

'Bad news, son,' he said softly. 'Your Uncle Ben has been shot.'

Peter found himself breathing heavily. 'Uncle Ben...' he whispered. 'No. No! It can't be!'

He grabbed the cop's arms. 'Who did it?' Peter yelled. 'Who shot him?'

The officer shook his head. 'It was a burglar—your uncle surprised him.'

The policeman looked grim. 'But don't worry, we've got him trapped. He's in an abandoned warehouse. We'll get him.'

He patted Peter's arm. 'Your aunt is next door—the neighbours are looking after her.'

'I've got to go,' Peter muttered, running upstairs.

He climbed out his bedroom window and onto the roof. He still had his costume on under his street clothes. He pulled on his mask.

A few minutes later,

Peter was on a building overlooking the warehouse. There were police cars all around it, and bright lights shining.

Peter heard a police captain say to one of his officers, 'He's in there...somewhere. But he'll pick us off like flies if we charge him.'

The longer they waited, though, the more likely the criminal would get away.

Not a chance, Peter thought to himself. And he realized he didn't just want Uncle Ben's killer caught—he wanted to be the one to catch him.

But how? With the police everywhere, he

couldn't just walk in. And there was nowhere for him to attach a web and swing in.

Peter decided he was going to have to try to jump from one building to the other.

Peter got a big running start, then pushed off the edge of the roof. He jumped as hard as he could.

It was enough—just barely. Peter grabbed the corner of the warehouse roof and pulled himself up. There were holes in the roof. *Not good for keeping rain out,* he thought. *But perfect for letting Spider-Man in.*

CHAPTER 10

Peter heard someone moving down on the second floor. *That's him,* he thought. *That's the man who took my uncle away.*

He crept across the ceiling until he found a staircase. He crawled down the staircase wall. He wanted to run as fast as he could, but forced himself to go slowly. He didn't want anyone to know someone else was in the warehouse: not the police and certainly not the killer.

Peter stopped when he got the second floor. It was very dark in most of the warehouse. The lights the police were shining made some parts very bright, but cast lots of large shadows. Where was the man?

Then Peter heard him. 'All I gotta do,' the man was muttering to himself. 'Is hold 'em off 'til the moon goes down. Then I ought to be able to slip away in the dark. Gotta escape. Just gotta escape.'

The man kept repeating himself. Peter moved across the ceiling towards the voice. Something about it sounded a little bit familiar. But that wasn't possible. Was it?

There was no time to think of that now. Peter found himself staring down at the man.

He was wearing a cap, so Peter couldn't see his face. But there was something about the leather jacket the man was wearing...what was it?

Peter pushed that thought out of his mind also. Suddenly, he was filled with anger. He was looking at the man who had shot his uncle.

He was in the same room as the man who had caused his uncle's death.

'You'll never escape again!'

Peter was surprised to hear those words. He was even more surprised when he realized they had come from his own mouth.

The killer was surprised too. He spun around, then around again, looking for whoever had just yelled.

But of course, he didn't see Peter. Because he didn't think to look up at the ceiling.

Peter couldn't help himself. He rushed down the wall towards the man.

Now the killer looked up. He was so startled to see someone crawling down a wall, headfirst, that he almost fell backwards. 'Huh?' the man gasped. 'What the—?'

'Surprised to see me?' Peter snarled. 'Now half as surprised as you're going to be!'

The man turned and tried to run away. 'Gotta...gotta get away!' he said to himself. 'I must be seein' things'!

Peter jumped off the wall and over the man's head. He landed in front of the man.

'There's no place on earth,' Peter growled, 'where you can hide from *me*.'

The man stumbled back. 'No no no...' he whimpered. 'This can't be happening. This can't be happening!'

He reached for his gun, but Peter was too fast. Before the man could get a shot off, Peter sent out a web. It covered the gun completely, and the man's hand.

The man looked down at his hand holding the gun, or tried to, but all he could see was a giant web.

He looked up to see Peter rushing towards him.

Peter punched the man in the face—it was

the first time he'd ever hit another person.

The man landed on the floor so hard he bounced. Peter ran over and pulled the man up, ready to hit him again if he needed to. But there was no need; the man was unconscious.

But Peter felt as if he'd just been punched in the stomach. 'No,' he whispered. He looked at the man again.

'That...that face...' he said to himself. 'It's... oh, no. It can't be. Please...no...'

Peter dropped the man back on the floor. He fell to his knees.

That's the man who ran past me at that lift, he thought. *The one I didn't stop when I had the chance.*

Peter didn't move for a long time. Finally, he wrapped the killer up in a web and hung him from a street light.

By the time the police discovered the killer

hanging outside the warehouse, Peter was a mile away. Sitting on a water tower, he stared up at the moon.

'My fault,' he said softly. 'All my fault. If only I had stopped him when I could have.'

Peter shook his head. 'But I didn't. And now…Uncle Ben…'

He pulled off his mask and buried his tear-stained face in his hands.

After a while, he sat up and wiped off his face. 'Aunt May is going to need me,' he said.

As Peter made his way home, he remembered something his Uncle Ben had once told him. Uncle Ben had usually been full of jokes, but this time he was very serious.

'Always remember, Peter,' his uncle had said, looking him in the eye, 'with great power comes great responsibility.'

Peter thought about that now. He didn't know why that spider had bitten him, why he had been the one it had happened to. But it had and he was. He had these amazing powers now.

And no matter how impossible it seemed, he was determined to do his best, so nobody else would feel the way he and Aunt May were feeling right now.

He would be a hero.

Spider-Man would be a hero.

For everyone.